Dedicated to Hazel Class 2021 and I
THE CONSTELLATIONS ABOVE!

ISBN: 9798513098249
Copyright: 2021 Gabriel St Aimee

Written by Gabriel St Aimee

Illustrated by Nataliia Mazepa

To Mally
Thank you for being awesome. You are part of my inspiration.

Gabriel 26/6/21
Your Year 3 teacher.

In the beginning there were millions
of stars in the dark night skies.
And all the people in all the towns loved the stars.
They told stories of the stars and made wishes upon them.

Eventually, the invention of bright glowing screens
brightened the night
skies and took away the people's love and
fascination with the stars.

Out of all the screen lovers,
Conner loved his screens the most.
Selfies, music, filters, video calls, games
– Oh, he loved playing games!
When he was asked to research
the stars and constellations for homework,
he stomped, pouted and fussed.
He was a boy who had absolutely no interest in stars.
Realising that he would lose his precious screens
if he didn't do it, he eventually did some research.
"Argh! What's the point!" he shouted.

His research told him that there were
millions of twinkling stars in the sky.
These stars could be connected
to make shapes or constellations.
Looking out of his 11th floor window
in the centre of town - he saw one lonely star.
Then he did the unthinkable.

He wished with all his might that the last remaining
star over Croydon and all others would disappear,
so he wouldn't have to do his pointless homework.
As soon as the words left his mouth,
the sky roared and the ground shook violently.
All the screens and street lamps went dark.

Conner tumbled across the skies,
through the clouds and
landed with a thud!
When he was finally able
to stand – he was surrounded
by a large crowd of peculiar,
glowing shapes.

They stared deeply.
They had not seen a human in a few
hundred years and they all wanted
 a look at this miniature being.
Conner for the first time in his
life was too stunned to speak.
The group was glowing brightly in excitement.
They were desperate to know so they asked,
"Do you recognise us?"

An ancient, bearded man spoke up,
"He doesn't know any of you.
In fact, he wants to erase all 88 constellations from
the sky to avoid doing his homework."
"You can't judge me! Constellations are just
random shapes,
they aren't interesting and they don't look like anything."

The bearded man continued,
"I can judge you and I will! You aren't in Croydon anymore!"
"I can see that! I don't want to know where I am,
just send me back!" demanded Conner.
Ancient, bearded man continued,
"I won't do that. You have been summoned
to the stars as a punishment for your crime against us.
Your punishment will be.."

Then a mighty, royal voice came.
"Oh Ptolemy, you brought him to worship and compliment
me every minute? You finally recognise my beauty!"
It was Cassiopeia, the vain queen.
She pushed her way to the front of the
crowd tossing the smaller figures to the ground.

Conner's eyes widened.
He was caught in Cassiopeia's gaze.
But he was stubborn.
He looked away and shouted,
"You don't look that great to me.
Why would anyone worship you?"

Cassiopeia replied,
"Anyone with eyes can see,
I am the most beautiful constellation.
Who else deserves to be worshiped?"
Ptolemy butted in quickly,
"Not so fast Cassiopeia!
I will give him till sunrise to pass my constellation test.
If he passes, he can return home."

„You must be able to grant every constellation
a wish that they ask you for,
in order to return home."
Ptolemy announced, with a smile.
"Woah! Woah! Woah! I'm not a genie.
How can I do that?" asked Conner.

"Well, you must truly listen to
the constellations and show an appreciation."
Conner knew that he was stuck.
He also knew that he wasn't great at tests and
had no desire to learn about
the constellations (never mind appreciate them).
He thought quickly. To boost his chance of escaping
he claimed boldly that he would only
grant wishes to the 3 strongest constellations.

"Fine, bring it on!" shouted the crowd.
Not wanting to take part in senseless fighting.
Half the constellations left.
The peace loving, animal type constellations
left the fighting and took a seat in the sky.
The remaining constellations seemed to be ready to battle.

BANG
SWOSH
POW

This epic battle frightened Conner.
It was clear that the constellations
were not just beautiful looking figures.
They were also dangerous.
The winners of the constellation
battle were Cassiopeia, Ursa Major and Orion.

Cassiopeia grabbed Conner first.

She pulled him by his ear and walked to her beautiful garden.
She laid on her sun lounger being fanned by servants.
For hours she asked and wished
for Conner to worship her and boasted
that her beauty was unmatched.

"If you don't grant my wish, you will be here forever,"
she announced.
"Just say, I'm more beautiful than any rose in this garden."
she boasted.
"Never! Your head is too big!"
Conner shouted then stuck out his tongue.
Conner stubbornly refused to grant her wish for hours.
Cassiopeia thought she was better than everyone else and
Conner didn't like that.

Time was passing quickly.
When it was clear that Connor would never grant the wish,
Ptolemy collected him.
"She is the vain queen; she is very proud.
Don't tell her, but, if you look closely at her constellation,
she is hanging upside down.
She is the only constellation which hang upside down.
It's her punishment from Zeus for saying
she is better looking than everyone and it's
amusing for the rest of us," explained Ptolemy.

Conner and Ptolemy both giggled as they
walked to find Ursa Major

Unlike Cassiopeia, she was not vain and not human.
Ursa was a bear...a BIG bear!
She was eating in the fields with a Little bear.
"There are loads of bears on Earth.
Are these special bears?" asked Conner
Ptolemy explained,
"Ursa Major and Ursa Minor are mother and son.
Zeus's wife was jealous of the
mother and turned her into a bear.
Zeus couldn't turn the mother back to a human
so he changed the son into a bear.
Now, they live happily together.

"That's terrible!
Zeus should find a way to change them back!"
demanded Conner.

When Conner approached, Ursa Major growled.
"What do I look like?" questioned Ursa Major.
"A... bear," Conner replied nervously.
"Exactly! People often call us Big Dipper and Little Dipper.
We are not dippers!
No one dips us! My wish is for you to go back and
tell people we are bears! Everyone should know this."
Saddened by the story of the Ursa Major and Ursa Minor,
Conner agreed, smiled reassuringly
and vowed to correct everyone.

Next was Orion - best hunter trained
by the Goddess of hunting.
The sky was steadily growing brighter
as Conner searched for Orion.
Conner looked and looked for Orion,
eventually finding him high up in a tree.
"Do you see a scorpion down there?"
Orion half-shouted, half-whispered.

""Nope, just bushes and dirt down here," replied Conner.

Orion wished for Conner to go hunting with him and make
sure scorpions didn't creep up and sting him.
But every time the grass swished Orion
would jump out of his skin.

Conner was not concerned with
Orion behaving more
like a bag of nervousness than a famous hunter.
Orion was his kind of constellation.
He was excited for an adventure,
crawling in the dirt and hiding behind bushes.
They spent the remaining time
hunting for doves in the woodland.
They caught nothing and saw no scorpions.

Just as the first rays of light crawled over the horizon,
Ptolemy appeared again.
Ptolemy began to explain Orion's back story,
"When he was on Earth, Orion set out to
hunt every animal on Earth.
One of the gods didn't like that
plan and sent a scorpion to end Orion's life.
Zeus placed Orion in the sky
as a constellation after his death.
There is also a scorpion constellation behind
Orion, so now he lives in constant fear of being stung."

Conner began to cry.
"I feel bad for how I treated the constellations.
I'm ready for your punishment since
I didn't grant all three wishes".
Ptolemy said to Conner,
"You didn't fail the test. I can tell from your tears that you have
developed an appreciation and understanding of the stars.
You don't want them to disappear anymore, do you?"
Conner shook his head.

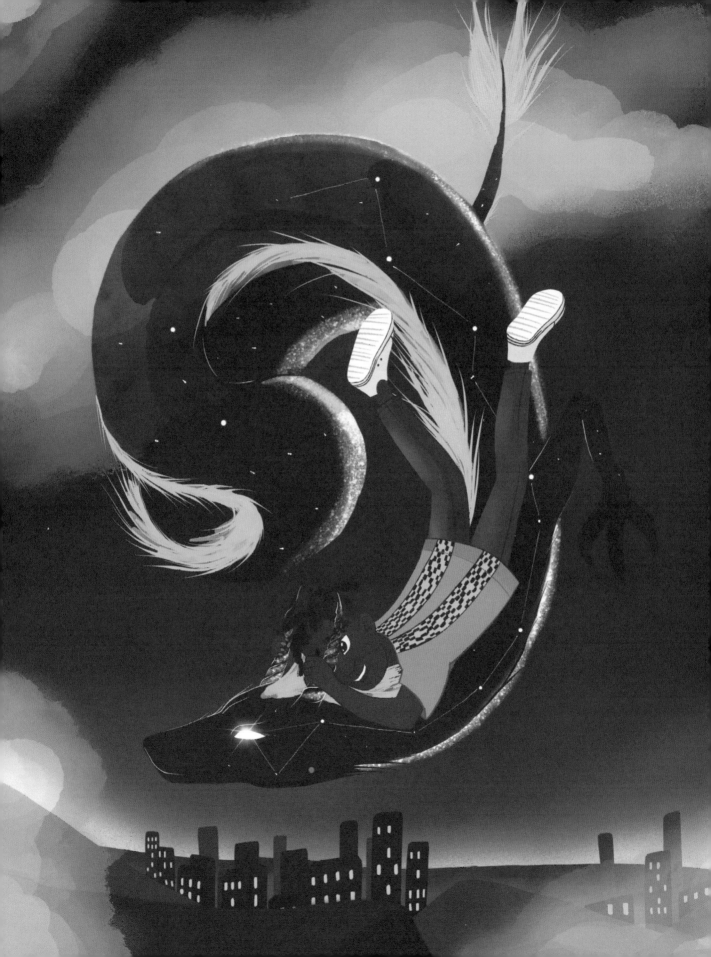

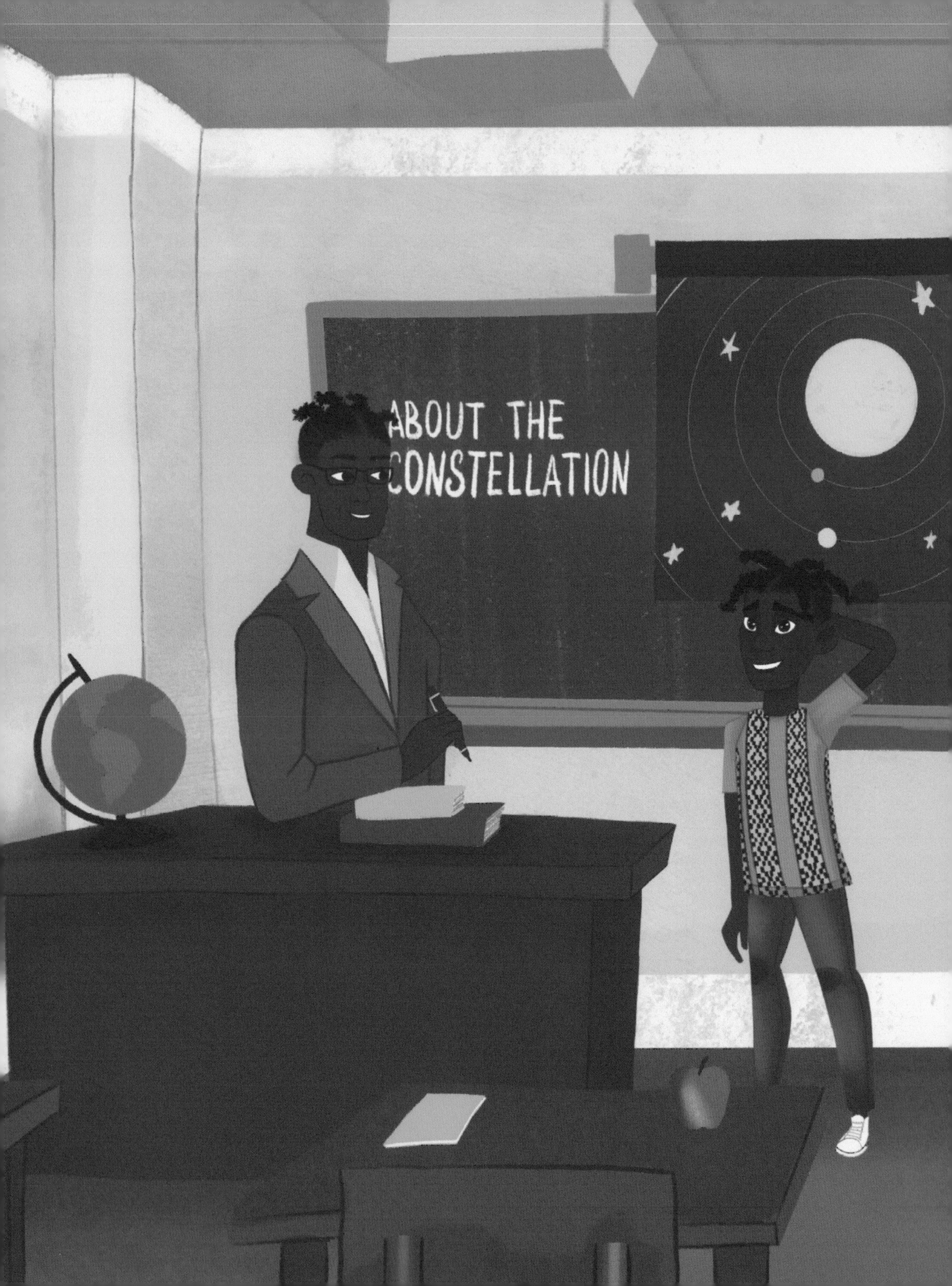
ABOUT THE
CONSTELLATION

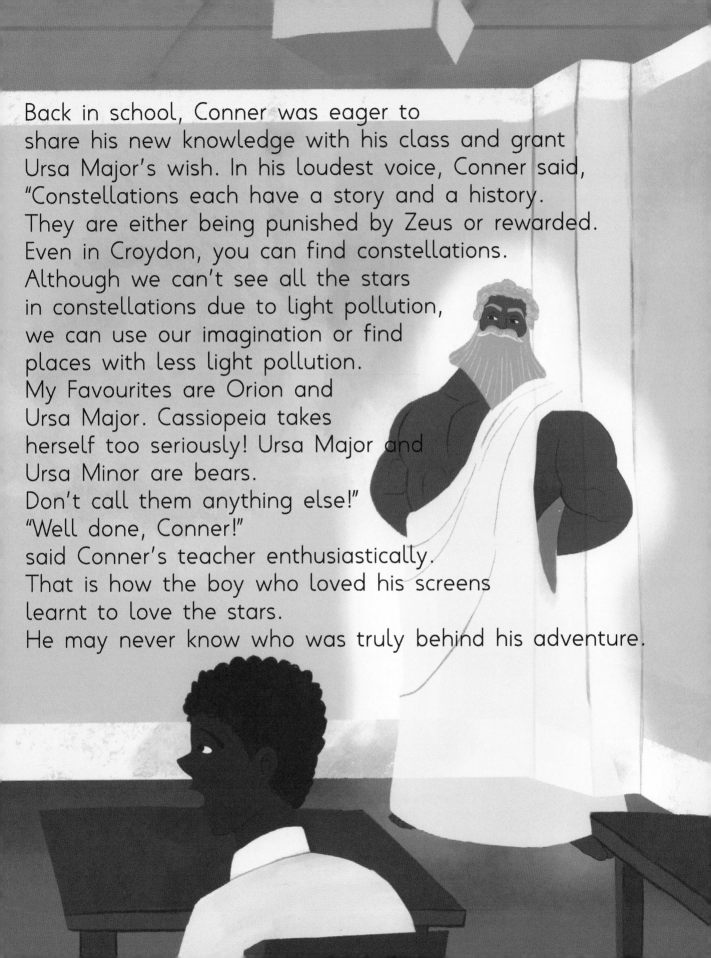

Back in school, Conner was eager to
share his new knowledge with his class and grant
Ursa Major's wish. In his loudest voice, Conner said,
"Constellations each have a story and a history.
They are either being punished by Zeus or rewarded.
Even in Croydon, you can find constellations.
Although we can't see all the stars
in constellations due to light pollution,
we can use our imagination or find
places with less light pollution.
My Favourites are Orion and
Ursa Major. Cassiopeia takes
herself too seriously! Ursa Major and
Ursa Minor are bears.
Don't call them anything else!"
"Well done, Conner!"
said Conner's teacher enthusiastically.
That is how the boy who loved his screens
learnt to love the stars.
He may never know who was truly behind his adventure.

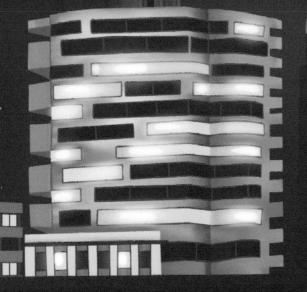

DRACO

URSA
MINOR

LYNX

CAMELOPARDALIS

CANCER

LEO

Printed in Great Britain
by Amazon